Sally Sore Loser

A Story About Winning and Losing

ECO-FRIENDLY BOOKS
Made in the USA

FSC
www.fsc.org
MIX
Paper from
responsible sources
FSC® C002589

To Mom and Dad with love.
To Kristine and Sarah, my editors, many heartfelt thanks — FJS

Published by
MAGINATION PRESS
An Educational Publishing Foundation Book
American Psychological Association
750 First Street, NE
Washington, DC 20002

For more information about our books, including a complete catalog,
please write to us, call 1-800-374-2721, or visit our website at
www.apa.org/pubs/magination.

Printed by Worzalla, Stevens Point, WI
Book design by Susan K. White

Library of Congress Cataloging-in-Publication Data
Sileo, Frank J., 1967–
  Sally Sore Loser : a story about winning and losing / by Frank J. Sileo ;
illustrated by Cary Pillo.
      p. cm.
  Summary: After having her classmates walk away from her during a soccer
game at recess because she hogs the ball, is bossy, and cares only about
winning, Sally gets some good advice from her teacher and her mother.
Includes note to parents.
  ISBN 978-1-4338-1189-0 (hardcover : alk. paper) —
ISBN 978-1-4338-1190-6 (pbk. : alk. paper)
[1. Sportsmanship—Fiction. 2. Behavior—Fiction.]
I. Pillo, Cary, ill. II. Title.
  PZ7.S582Sal 2012
  [Fic]—dc23   2012009429

Manufactured in the United States of America

10 9 8 7 6 5 4 3 2 1

Sally Sore Loser

A Story About Winning and Losing

by Frank J. Sileo, PhD

illustrated by
Cary Pillo

MAGINATION PRESS • WASHINGTON, DC
American Psychological Association

Sally loves to play games.

Sally loves sports.

Sally loves to be
first in line.

Sally likes to finish her macaroni and cheese before her brother.

Sally loves to be first out the door at recess.

Sally loves to win, and she hates to lose.

One day during recess,
Sally and her classmates
were playing a game of soccer.

During the game, Sally was hogging the ball as usual.

When her team was losing
by three points she screamed,

**"Do you want to be a bunch of losers?
Let's win!!"**

Emma said to Sally, "Stop being so bossy!
Who cares if we win or lose? It's just a game!"

Sally snapped at Emma,
"Well, I don't like to lose! Winning is the most important thing in the world!"

During the game,
all the kids walked away
from Sally.

Sally screamed,

**"Where is
everyone going?
We didn't finish
playing!"**

"We don't want to play with you anymore, Sally.
We are going to play somewhere else," Carlos said.

"You're not fun to play with," Diane told Sally.

"You are Sally Sore Loser!" Jeremy shouted at Sally.
Sally began to cry and sat in the middle of the field.

After recess, Sally's teacher, Mr. Taylor, spoke to her. "I know everyone wants to win at games. It's okay to feel disappointed when we lose. But when we act like a sore loser, other kids don't want to play with us. When we play games or sports all we need to do is try our best and have fun.

Let's review the rules for being a good sport."

Being a Good Sport

1. Be polite to your teammates and the opposite team.
2. Cool down when you get upset.
3. Don't show off or hog the ball.
4. Don't argue with a teacher, teammate, opponent, or referee.
5. Know the rules of the game.
6. Be fair to everyone.
7. Never, ever cheat.
8. Try your best and have fun!

"A bad loser or sore loser can get angry, frustrated, or sad about losing. They may also be bossy and bully their teammates. They may cheat or argue with their friends and the grown-ups," Mr. Taylor said.

Mr. Taylor explained, "Bad winners brag and tease others about losing."

Sally thought about a time when she was playing a video game
with her friend Ava and laughed at her for losing.
After the game she shouted out,

"I am the best video game player ever!"

"Sore losers and bad winners win nothing
and they can lose their friends," Mr. Taylor told Sally.

The next morning,
Sally did not eat her breakfast.
She kept pushing her cereal around her bowl.
She kept hearing "Sally Sore Loser"
over and over in her mind.

"What's wrong, Sally?" her mom said.

"The kids were mean to me yesterday. They didn't want to play with me at recess and they called me a name."

"What did they call you?"

"They called me Sally Sore Loser. Mr. Taylor told me that bad losers and bad winners never win anything and they can lose friends."

"Mr. Taylor gave you excellent advice, Sally. Here is something for you to do and remember today at school. I want you to think of all the fun things about playing games, like being outside, being with your friends, and laughing with others."

"But if you are starting to lose at a game,
I want you to take a deep breath,
let it out slowly, and say to yourself…

I've won if I had fun."

At recess that day, all the kids started to play a game of kickball.

When Diane missed the ball three times, Sally wanted to scream, but instead she took deep breaths to calm down.

She called out,

"**Good try!**"

When one of her teammates kicked the ball,
it went out of bounds.
The other kids were arguing about it.
She said, "Instead of arguing,
how about we have a do-over?"

When it was
Sally's turn to kick the ball,
she got to first base
but was tagged out.
She started to cry but thought,

"I've won if I've had fun."

The recess bell rang.
Sally's team had lost.
Jeremy came up to Sally and said,
"Good game. You weren't a sore loser today."

Sally said,

"Thanks. It's still hard to lose, but I won because I had fun!"

Note to Parents

Good sportsmanship and learning how to play well with others are important skills to teach children on and off the field. "Being a good sport" is not an innate skill. Beginning in early childhood, children need to learn how to share, follow rules, handle emotions, try their best, and win and lose with respect, dignity, and graciousness. Being a good sport applies not only to athletics but also to other areas of a child's life. Children may need to learn to cope with losing the lead in the school play, getting a lower mark on an exam or paper as compared to their peers, losing a video game, or not getting a solo in the choir, to name a few.

Showing good sportsmanship is not always easy for children, or even adults. No one likes to lose. It is natural for children to feel sad, disappointed, and even angry. It is how children act on those feelings that determines good sportsmanship. It is hard to congratulate the winning team, to accept questionable calls by referees with a calm demeanor, or to congratulate the person who got the part in the school play that you wanted, for example. Boys and girls who struggle with losing can learn skills to help them become good sports, as Sally does in the story.

The Importance of Being a Good Sport

Learning to display good sportsmanship benefits children in many ways. We live in a very competitive society and the pressures imposed on children are tremendous. Children who are poor losers often are found bullying in the classroom or in other social situations, having received the message that winning or having power over others is everything. With bullying being such a problem in our world today, teaching good sportsmanship becomes even more important. When children learn to cope with losing, we can encourage them to work harder, to change or re-evaluate goals, and to persevere in the face of adversity. Learning how to accept losing can prepare them for potential losses and disappointments in the future. It can help build character, humility, and perseverance.

Like poor losers, poor winners often lose the respect of their peers and may consequently lose friends. They may come across as conceited, boastful, unkind, and argumentative. Children who focus too much on winning often forget that they are involved in an activity to have fun. On the other hand, good winners have been found to be generous, in that they view winning as a team effort and consequently work better with others. They may also show more gratitude toward their parents, coaches, and teachers for helping them achieve their goals. Good winners can also be humble, have a healthier perspective on the activity, and engage in better peer relations.

Modeling Good Sportsmanship

As adults we can often get caught up in winning as well. Let's face it—winning feels good. However, when this is the primary focus of coaches, parents, and others, children get the message that they are only good and worthwhile if they win. As adults, we function as role models for our children on how to be a good sport. When we emphasize good sportsmanship, such as playing with others in a fair manner, sharing, having fun, honing skills, and being a good team player, we help kids develop tools for interacting well with others.

When children win or lose, it is necessary to allow them to express whatever emotion they experience. It is completely understandable for them to feel disappointed, angry, and sad when they lose, just as it is reasonable for them to feel happy, proud, and excited when they win. As the adults in their lives, it is our responsibility to listen to and help them process their feelings, and to limit any acting out such as pouting, name calling, temper tantrums, destruction of property, and physical violence. In addition, adults need to model appropriateness when their children win or lose at something. Shouting at players on the field, yelling at the child from the sidelines, speaking to children in a derogatory manner, and screaming at coaches, referees, or other adults in charge may further hinder the child in developing good sportsmanship. As adults, we need to be good sports, too!

Teaching Children to Be Good Winners and Good Losers

How can we as adults nurture good sportsmanship in our children? Here are some suggestions, whether the activity is a sport, video game, dance recital, school play, or an academic competition:

- Remember that you are your child's role model. Be mindful of what you say at an event and at home. Be careful not to yell at, belittle, or be overly critical of your children or others' children. Teach your children ways to improve their skills and to play fairly. Encourage them to do and be their best!

- Do not engage in bad-mouthing of coaches, teachers, directors, or referees. If you have a problem with the way things are handled, speak privately with these adults. If we demonstrate respect for those in authority, then our children learn to show them respect as well.

- Be a good spectator and teach your child to do the same. Cheer for every player on the team, not just your child. Your child may not always be the star or the one who starts in the game.

- Don't try to live your dreams or your favorite pastimes through your children. In order for them to be happy they have to be themselves and not you. Help them to find their unique interests, talents, and abilities and celebrate them.

- Always encourage your child to say positive things to others such as "Good game!" "Congratulations!" and "Nice job!" When playing games or engaging in other activities with your child, model other aspects of being a good sport such as taking turns, congratulating successes, and being empathetic to losses. If your child begins to argue, cheat, or act out in other ways, address these behaviors immediately and remind him about the aspect of fun and that winning is not everything.

- Teach your child to show gratitude. She won a game or got a part in a school play because of the help of a coach, a voice teacher, a dance instructor, or you, her parent. Help her to see that her success may be a result of the support and guidance given by others.

- Set an example by congratulating the parents and children on the opposing team and encourage your child to do the same. If your child should win, teach him to be humble and not to brag or taunt the other team.

- Don't forget about the fun. If it's not fun, why do it? Activities that involve good sportsmanship aren't always about winning and losing. They're about making and keeping friends, learning skills, keeping our bodies healthy, building character, and making memories. Even if children are not good at something, it doesn't mean they are not having fun doing it and feeling good about themselves as a result. After a game, you can say to your child, "I loved watching you play" or "It was great seeing you have so much fun in the game." These statements deemphasize winning and losing, and remind your child she is in it to have fun.

- Look for opportunities to talk about good sportsmanship in professional athletes, actors, and Olympians, to name a few. Movies that have a sports or competitive theme can also help foster conversations about sportsmanship. You may say, "When the coach was screaming at the referee, it looked like he was being a poor sport. What could the coach have done differently?" Similarly, when players are shaking hands after a game you can point out good sportsmanship by saying, "Despite losing, the players still congratulated the other team."

- Understand that we do not build self-esteem by giving children an award for everything. It is important to teach children that they may lose at things in life and how to handle losing. If your child is not succeeding in a certain hobby or activity, encourage him to work harder or try something else. Focus on the effort made by your child. Do not permit your child to quit an activity because things are not going well right away. This will encourage your child to give up when things don't work out according to his plan. Children who are poor losers typically give up easily and want to quit if they are not winning or see that they might lose at a game. If your child feels discouraged and wants to quit you may say something like, "Playing a sport takes a lot of hard work and practice. Before giving up and quitting the team, let's practice your batting skills. Even professional athletes need to practice. Maybe if you hang in there, you will get better. If after some practice you still feel this isn't the sport for you, then we can think about doing a different activity that you may enjoy." If your child wants to quit in the middle of an activity you may say, "You wanted to play this game. I think it would be a good idea to finish what we started. Once we finish this game, we can play something else."

We need to remember, as adults, that we did not always get our first job, our college of choice, our first love, our dream home or car. If we did, perhaps we were fortunate. When we start early and teach children that life is filled with losing and winning, we help them develop resilience, a more positive self-image, and a healthier outlook on life.

Reading this book with your child can be an effective way to convey important lessons. Sally's story can be a starting point for discussing good and poor sportsmanship with your child. As you read the story, you may ask your child what Sally and her teammates may be feeling or what behaviors they are displaying, for example. You can also discuss when Sally is being a poor sport, and when she is demonstrating the "Rules for Being a Good Sport," like encouraging her teammates, reminding herself to have fun, and being flexible with questionable calls during a game.

You are the best resource for teaching your child about sportsmanship. However, if your child continues to act out after losing or demonstrate poor winning behavior, it may be time to seek consultation and evaluation from a licensed psychologist or psychotherapist.

About the Author

Frank J. Sileo, PhD, is a New Jersey licensed psychologist and the executive director of the Center for Psychological Enhancement, LLC in Ridgewood, New Jersey. Dr. Sileo received his doctorate in psychology from Fordham University in New York City. He is the author of three other children's books, *Toilet Paper Flowers: A Story for Children About Crohn's Disease, Hold the Cheese Please! A Story for Children About Lactose Intolerance* and *Bug Bites and Campfires: A Story for Kids About Homesickness.* Dr. Sileo is an active public speaker and speaks across the country to children and families. He has been featured in psychological journals, newspapers, magazines, the web, radio, webcasts, and television. You can learn more about Dr. Sileo on his website, drfranksileo.com.

About the Illustrator

Cary Pillo grew up in a small town near the Cascade Mountains in Washington state, and now lives in Seattle with her husband and their dog, Atlas. She has illustrated many children's books, including *A Terrible Thing Happened, Gentle Willow, Striped Shirts and Flowered Pants,* and *Tibby Tried It.*